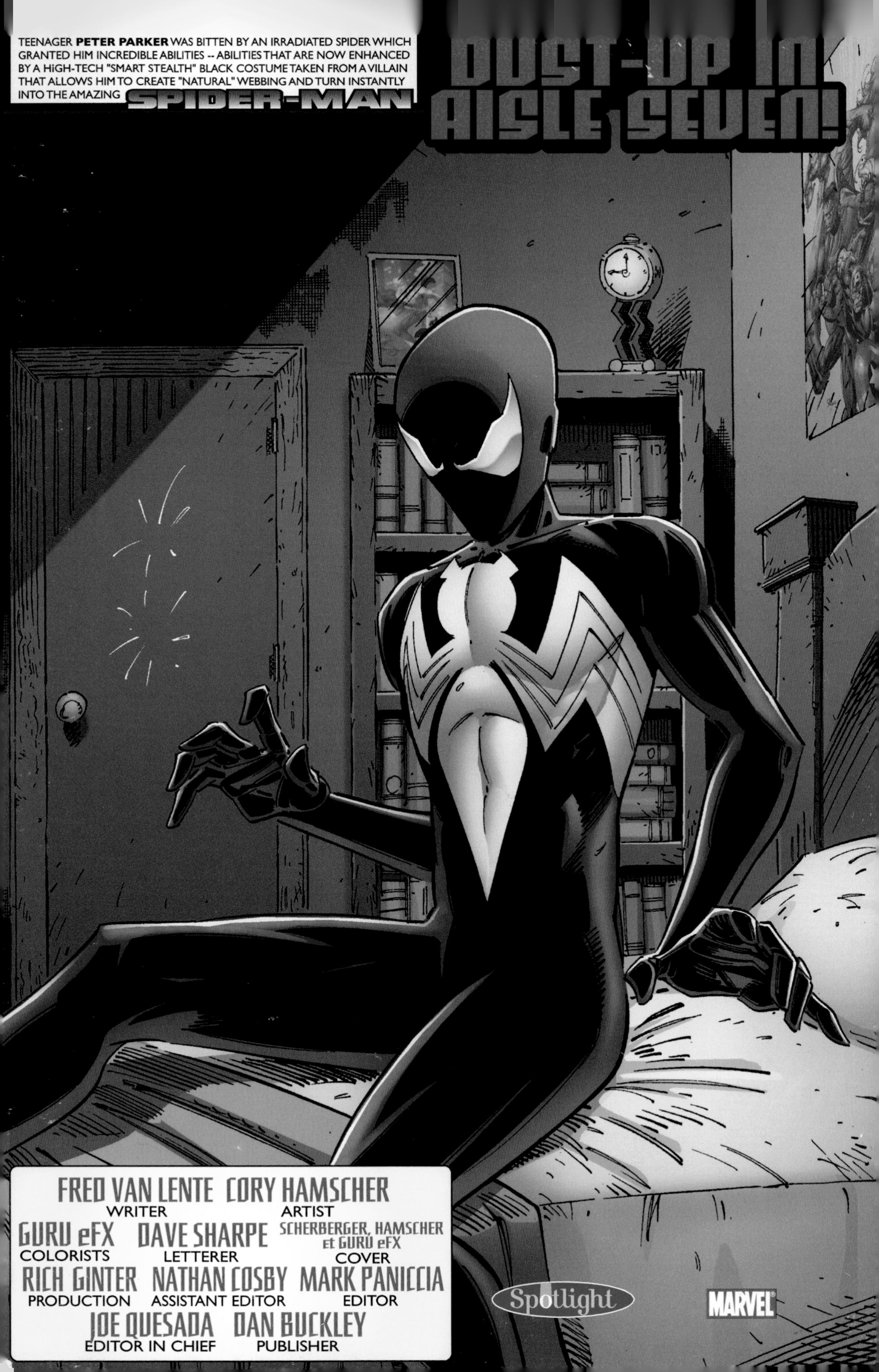
TEENAGER PETER PARKER WAS BITTEN BY AN IRRADIATED SPIDER WHICH GRANTED HIM INCREDIBLE ABILITIES -- ABILITIES THAT ARE NOW ENHANCED BY A HIGH-TECH "SMART STEALTH" BLACK COSTUME TAKEN FROM A VILLAIN THAT ALLOWS HIM TO CREATE "NATURAL" WEBBING AND TURN INSTANTLY INTO THE AMAZING SPIDER-MAN
DUST-UP IN AISLE SEVEN!
FRED VAN LENTE WRITER
CORY HAMSCHER ARTIST
GURU eFX COLORISTS
DAVE SHARPE LETTERER
SCHERBERGER, HAMSCHER et GURU eFX COVER
RICH GINTER PRODUCTION
NATHAN COSBY ASSISTANT EDITOR
MARK PANICCIA EDITOR
JOE QUESADA EDITOR IN CHIEF
DAN BUCKLEY PUBLISHER
Spotlight
MARVEL

VISIT US AT
www.abdopublishing.com

Reinforced library bound edition published in 2008 by Spotlight, a division of the ABDO Publishing Group, 8000 West 78th Street, Edina, Minnesota 55439. Spotlight produces high-quality reinforced library bound editions for schools and libraries. Published by agreement with Marvel Characters, Inc.

Library of Congress Cataloging-in-Publication Data

Van Lente, Fred.
  Dust-up in aisle seven! / Fred Van Lente, writer ; Cory Hamscher, artist ; GURU eFX, colorists ; Dave Sharpe, letterer.
     p. cm. -- (Spider-man)
  "Marvel age"--Cover.
  Revision of issue 23 of Marvel adventures Spider-man.
  ISBN 978-1-59961-394-9
  1. Graphic novels. I. Hamscher, Cory. II. Marvel adventures. Spider-man. 23. III. Title.

PN6728.S6V35 2008
809'.93351--dc22

                                        2007020242

All Spotlight books have reinforced library bindings and
are manufactured in the United States of America.

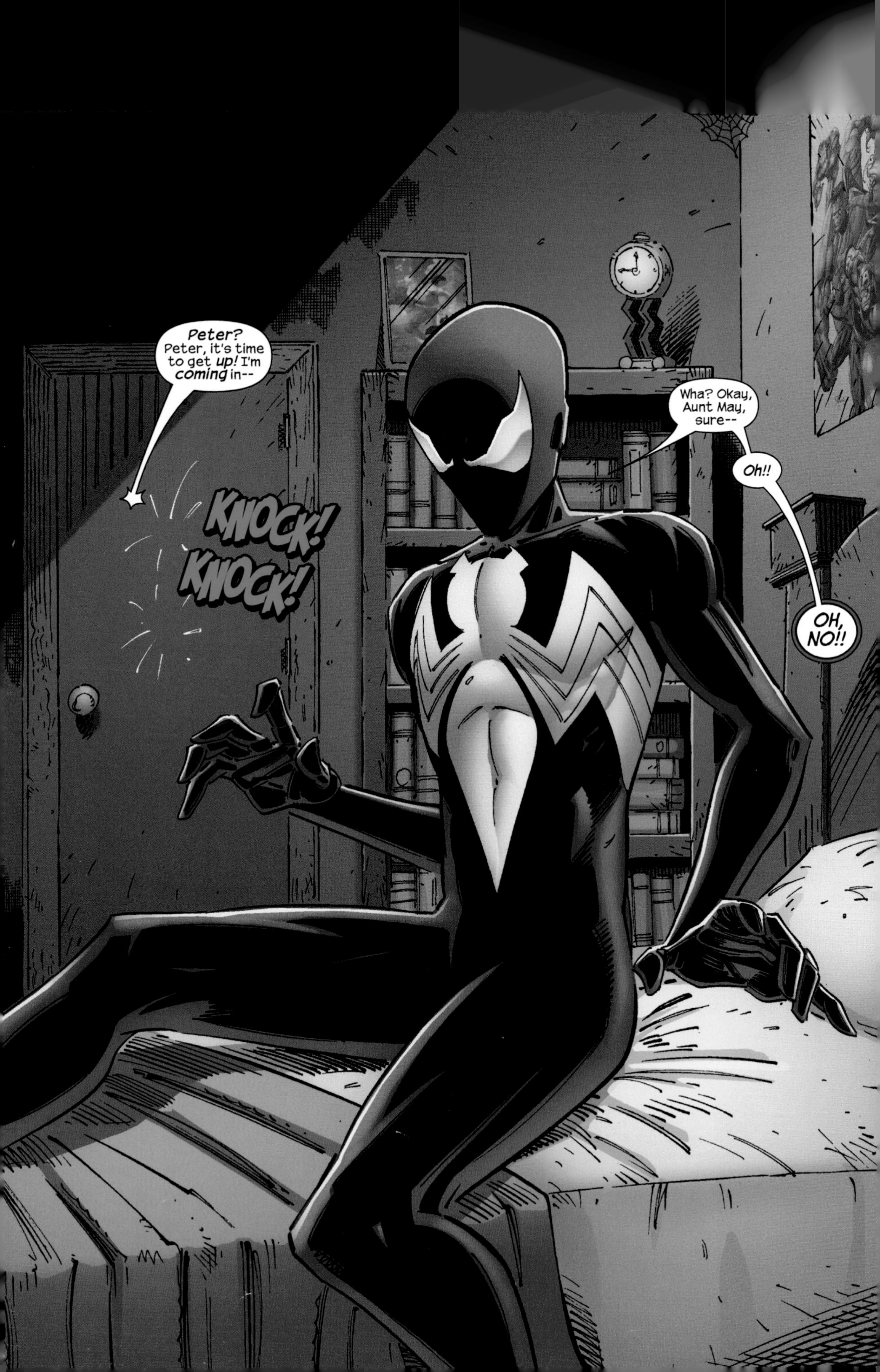
Peter? Peter, it's time to get up! I'm coming in--
KNOCK! KNOCK!
Wha? Okay, Aunt May, sure--
Oh!!
OH, NO!!

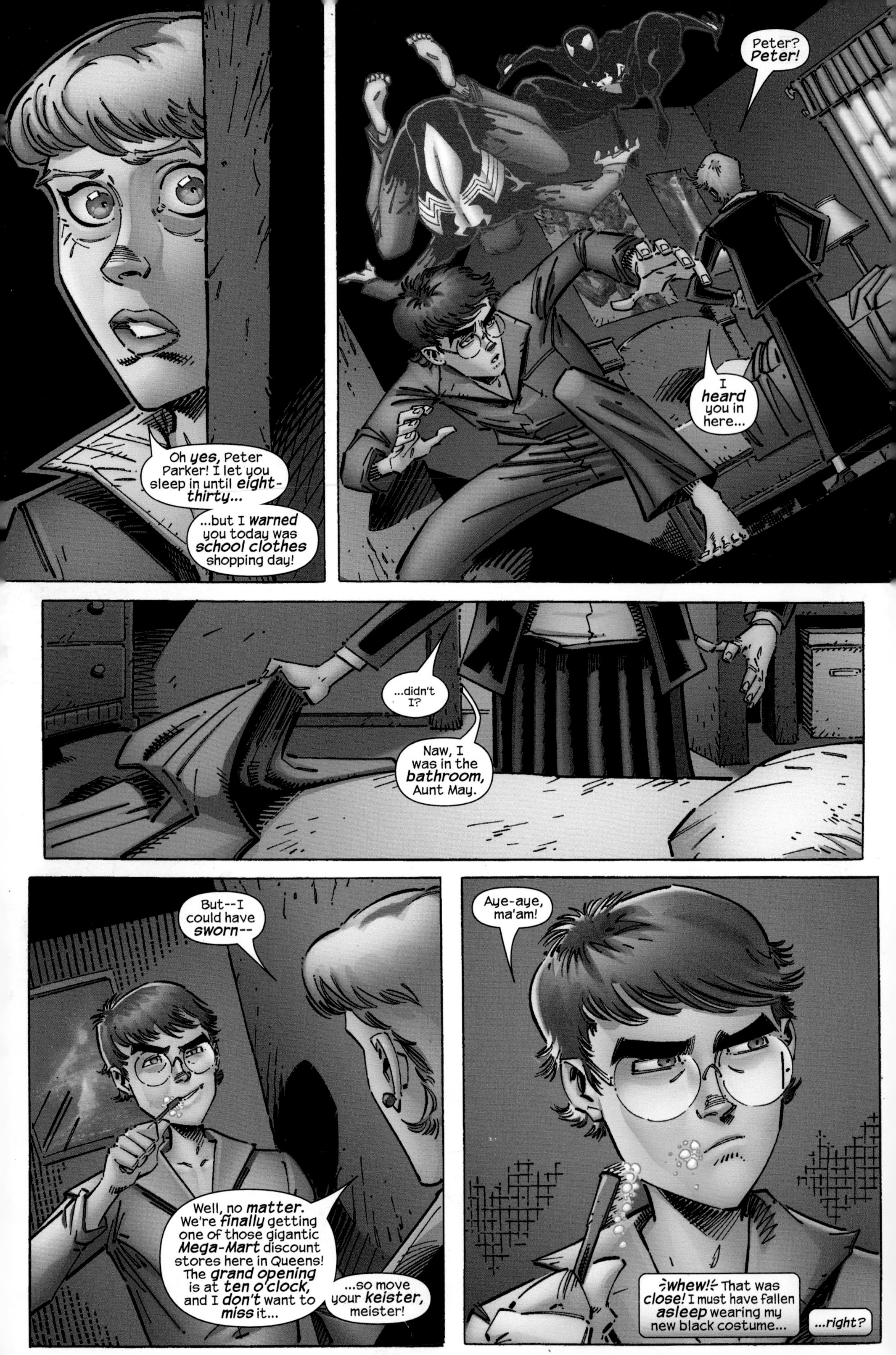
Oh yes, Peter Parker! I let you sleep in until eight-thirty...
...but I warned you today was school clothes shopping day!
Peter? Peter!
I heard you in here...
...didn't I?
Naw, I was in the bathroom, Aunt May.
But--I could have sworn--
Well, no matter. We're finally getting one of those gigantic Mega-Mart discount stores here in Queens! The grand opening is at ten o'clock, and I don't want to miss it...
...so move your keister, meister!
Aye-aye, ma'am!
whew! That was close! I must have fallen asleep wearing my new black costume...
...right?

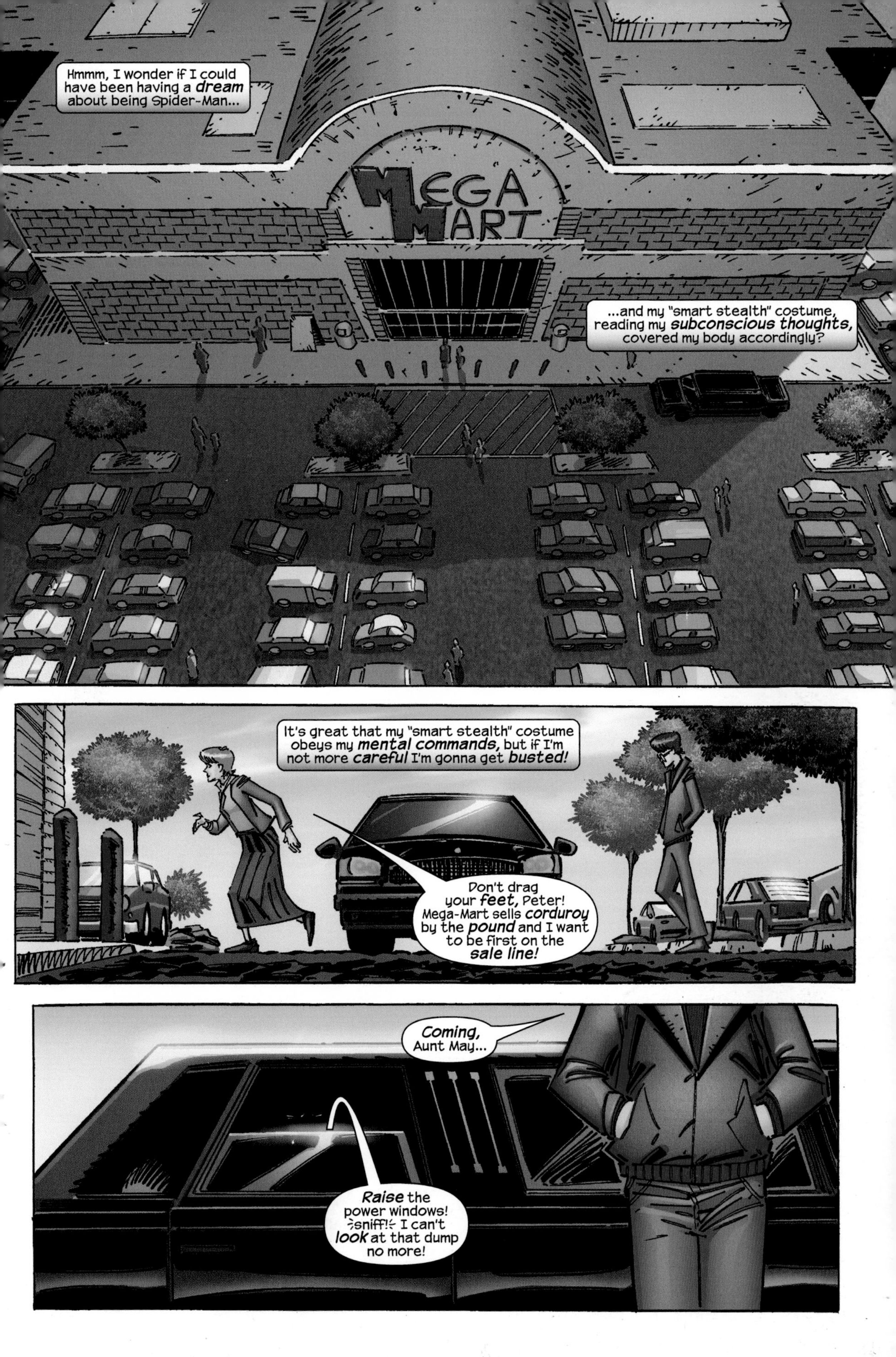

Hmmm, I wonder if I could have been having a dream about being Spider-Man...
MEGA MART
...and my "smart stealth" costume, reading my subconscious thoughts, covered my body accordingly?
It's great that my "smart stealth" costume obeys my mental commands, but if I'm not more careful I'm gonna get busted!
Don't drag your feet, Peter! Mega-Mart sells corduroy by the pound and I want to be first on the sale line!
Coming, Aunt May...
Raise the power windows! *sniff!* I can't look at that dump no more!

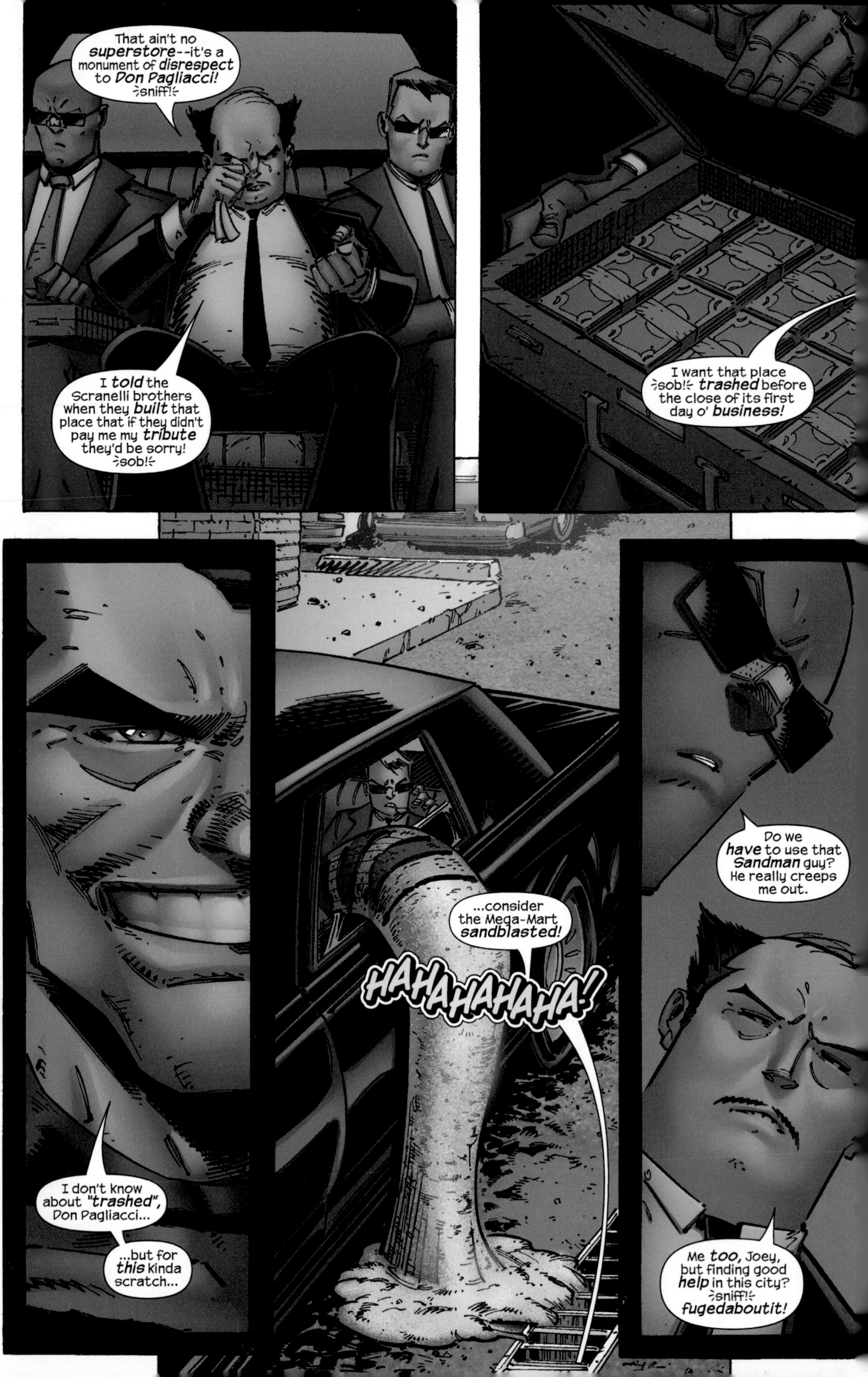
That ain't no superstore--it's a monument of disrespect to Don Pagliacci! ⊰sniff!⊱
I told the Scranelli brothers when they built that place that if they didn't pay me my tribute they'd be sorry! ⊰sob!⊱
I want that place ⊰sob!⊱ trashed before the close of its first day o' business!
I don't know about "trashed", Don Pagliacci...
...but for this kinda scratch...
...consider the Mega-Mart sandblasted!
HAHAHAHAHA!
Do we have to use that Sandman guy? He really creeps me out.
Me too, Joey, but finding good help in this city? ⊰sniff!⊱ fugedaboutit!

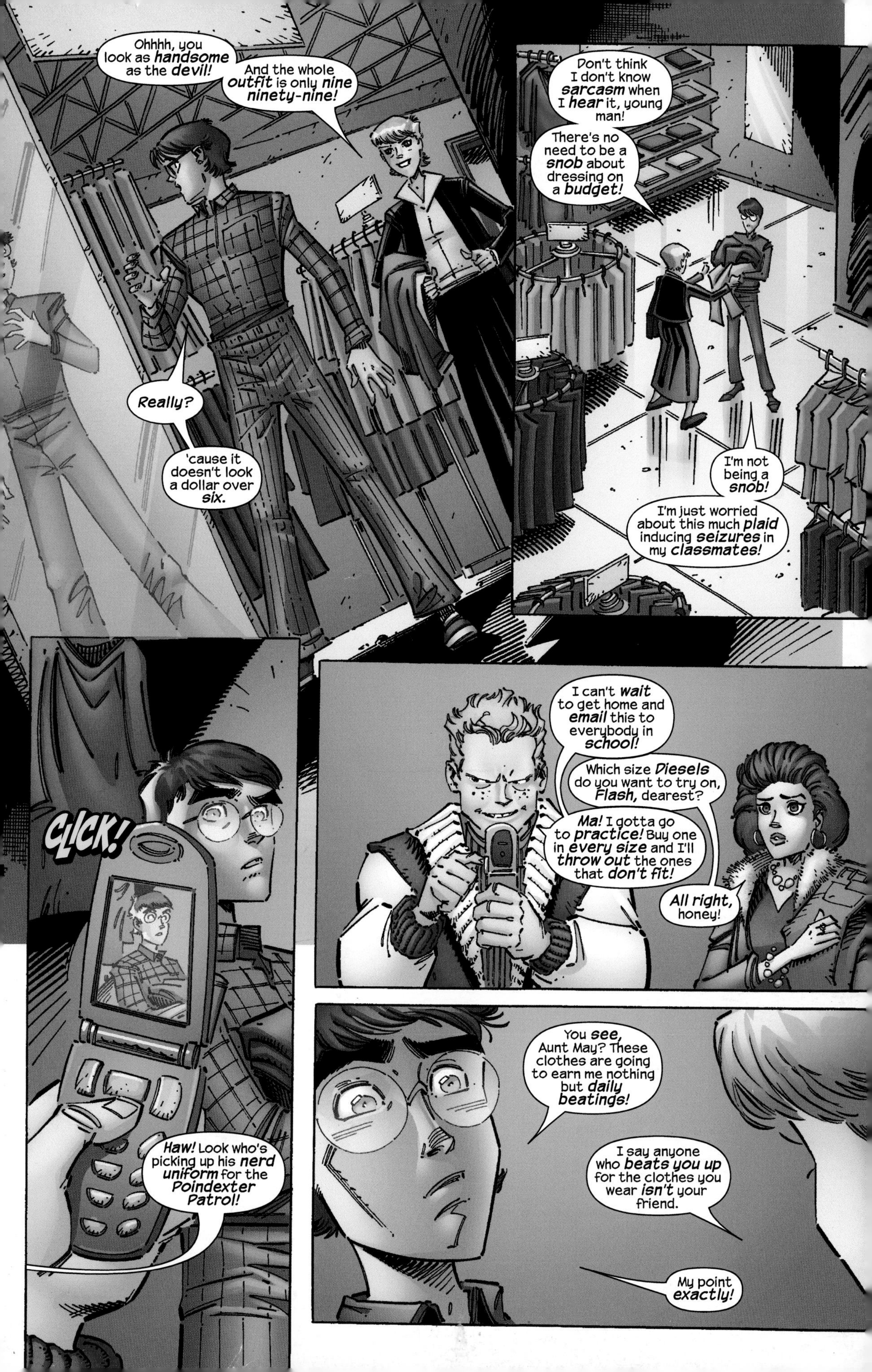
Ohhhh, you look as handsome as the devil!
And the whole outfit is only nine ninety-nine!
Really?
'cause it doesn't look a dollar over six.
Don't think I don't know sarcasm when I hear it, young man!
There's no need to be a snob about dressing on a budget!
I'm not being a snob!
I'm just worried about this much plaid inducing seizures in my classmates!
CLICK!
Haw! Look who's picking up his nerd uniform for the Poindexter Patrol!
I can't wait to get home and email this to everybody in school!
Which size Diesels do you want to try on, Flash, dearest?
Ma! I gotta go to practice! Buy one in every size and I'll throw out the ones that don't fit!
All right, honey!
You see, Aunt May? These clothes are going to earn me nothing but daily beatings!
I say anyone who beats you up for the clothes you wear isn't your friend.
My point exactly!

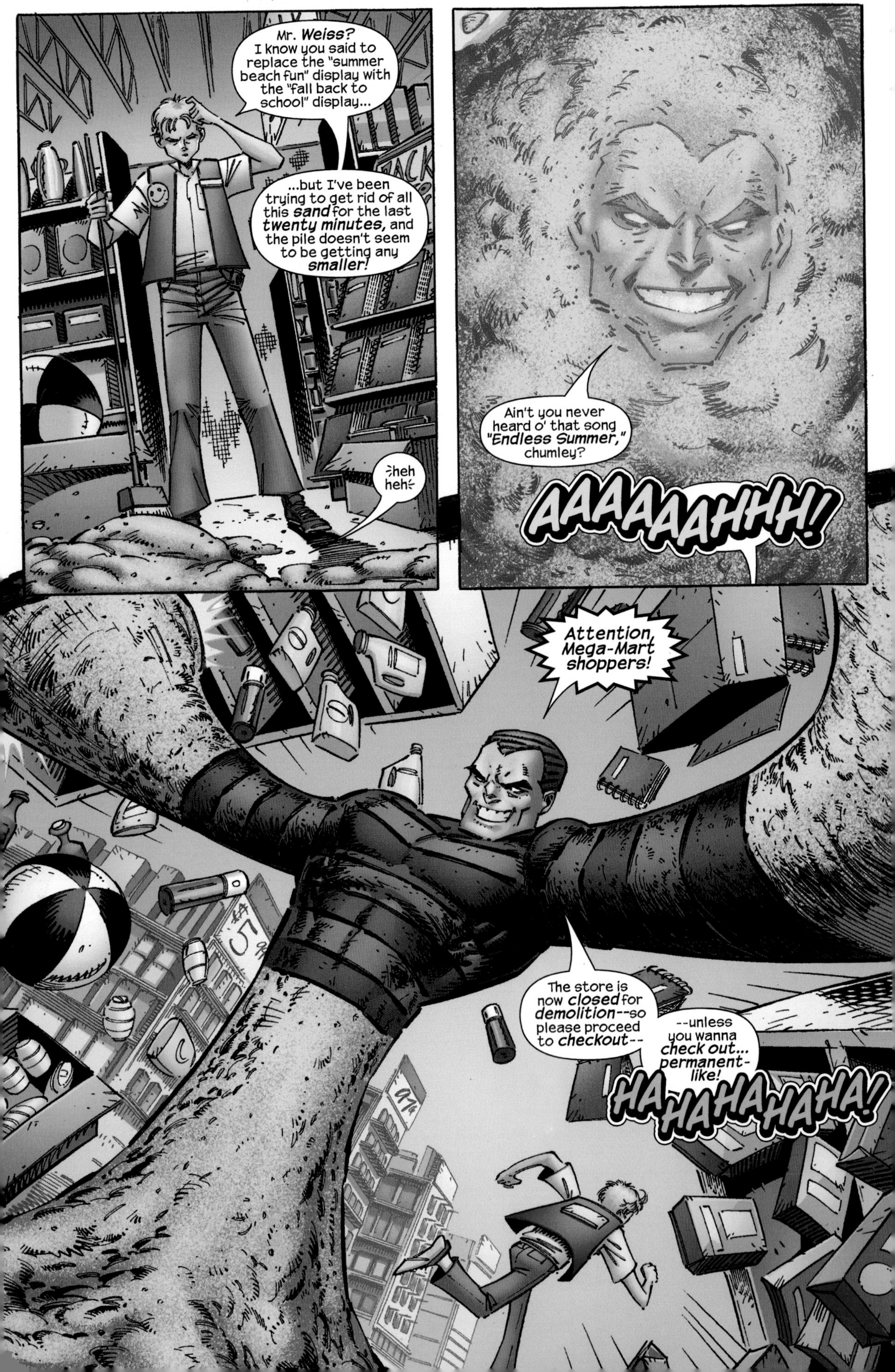

Mr. Weiss? I know you said to replace the "summer beach fun" display with the "fall back to school" display...
...but I've been trying to get rid of all this sand for the last twenty minutes, and the pile doesn't seem to be getting any smaller!
heh heh
Ain't you never heard o' that song "Endless Summer," chumley?
AAAAAAHHH!
Attention, Mega-Mart shoppers!
The store is now closed for demolition--so please proceed to checkout--
--unless you wanna check out... permanent-like!
HAHAHAHAHAHA!

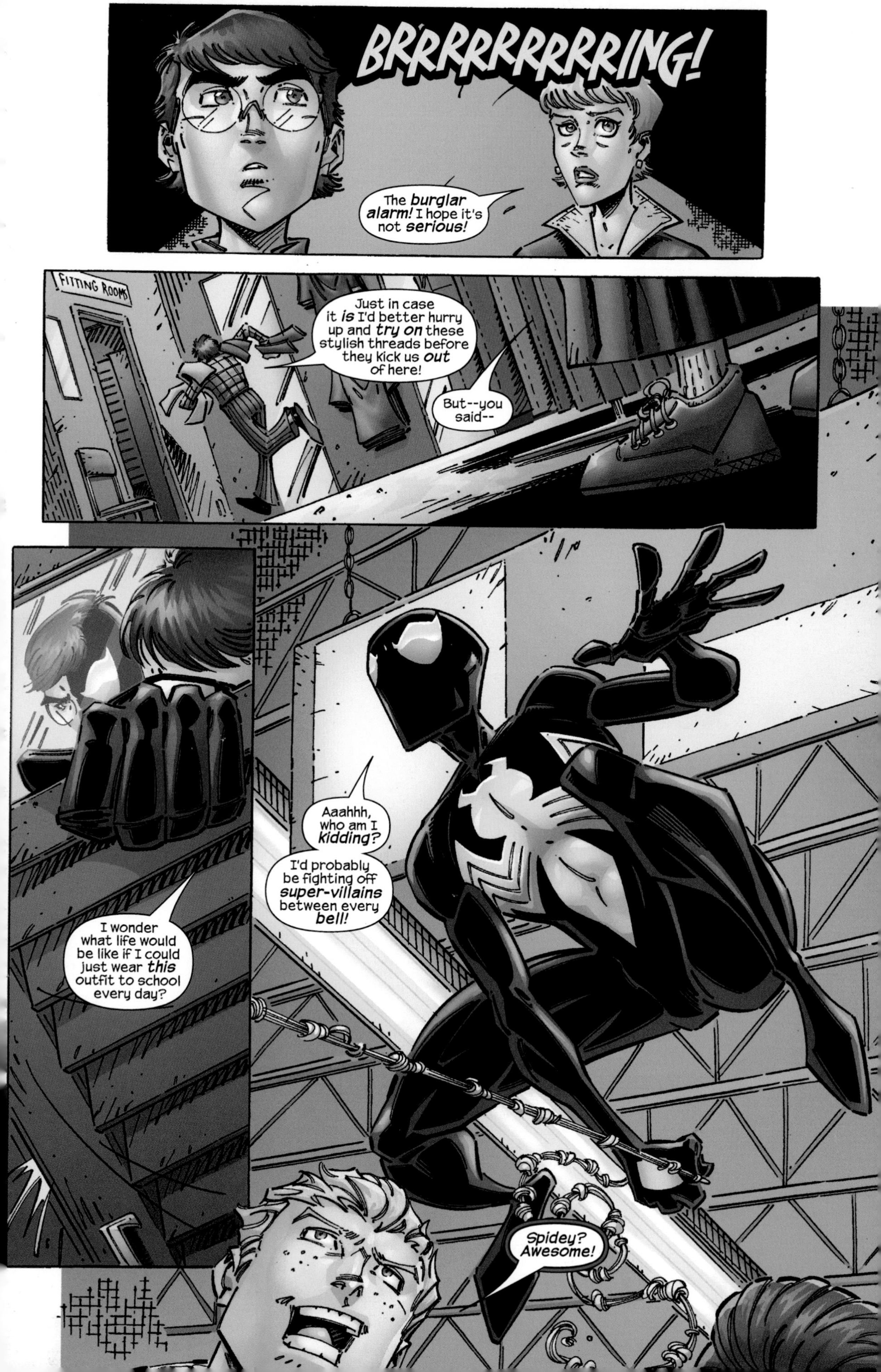
BRRRRRRRRRING!
The burglar alarm! I hope it's not serious!
FITTING ROOMS
Just in case it is I'd better hurry up and try on these stylish threads before they kick us out of here!
But--you said--
I wonder what life would be like if I could just wear this outfit to school every day?
Aaahhh, who am I kidding?
I'd probably be fighting off super-villains between every bell!
Spidey? Awesome!

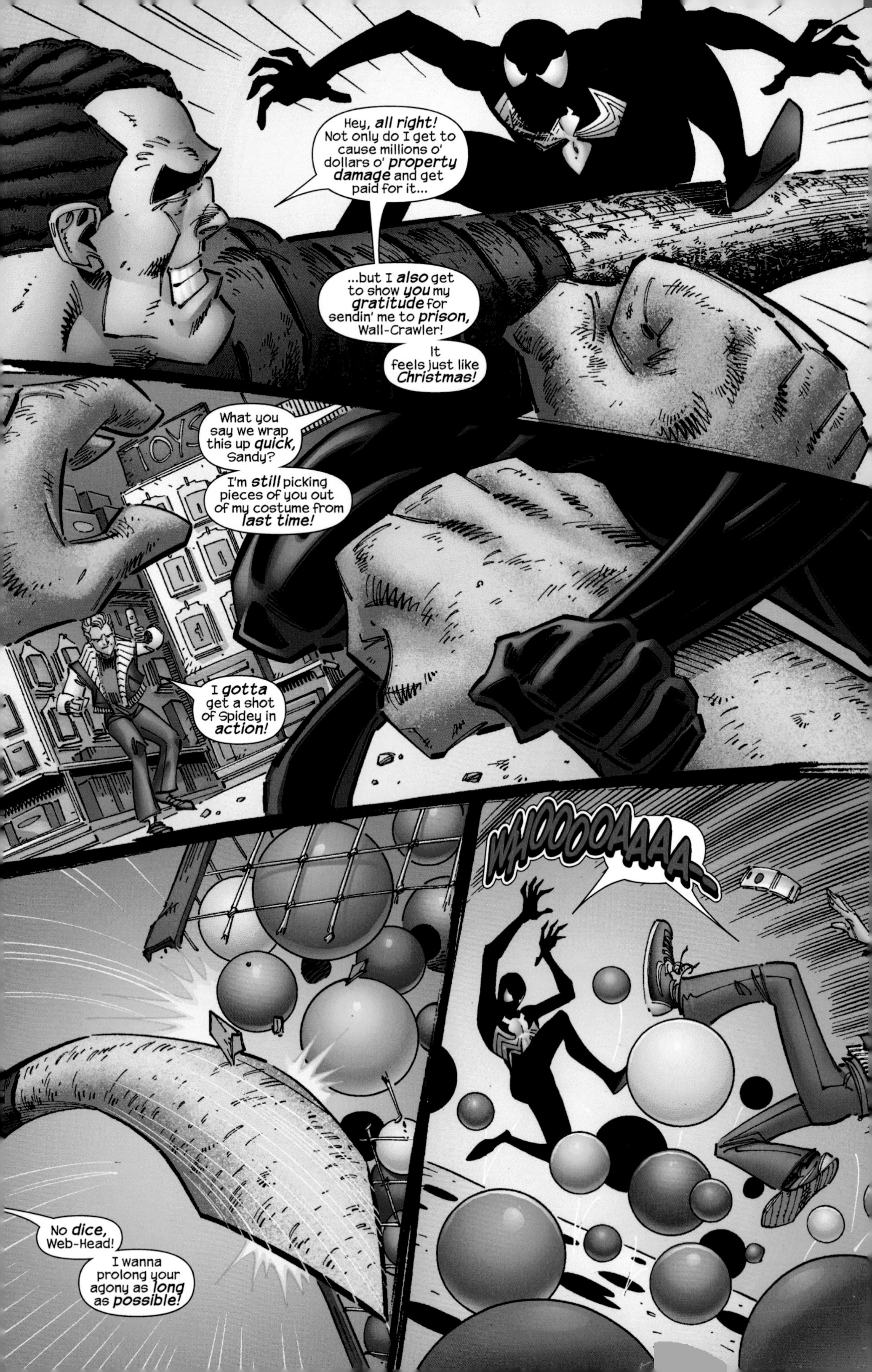

Hey, all right! Not only do I get to cause millions o' dollars o' property damage and get paid for it...
...but I also get to show you my gratitude for sendin' me to prison, Wall-Crawler!
It feels just like Christmas!
What you say we wrap this up quick, Sandy?
I'm still picking pieces of you out of my costume from last time!
TOYS
I gotta get a shot of Spidey in action!
WHOOOOOAAAA-
No dice, Web-Head!
I wanna prolong your agony as long as possible!

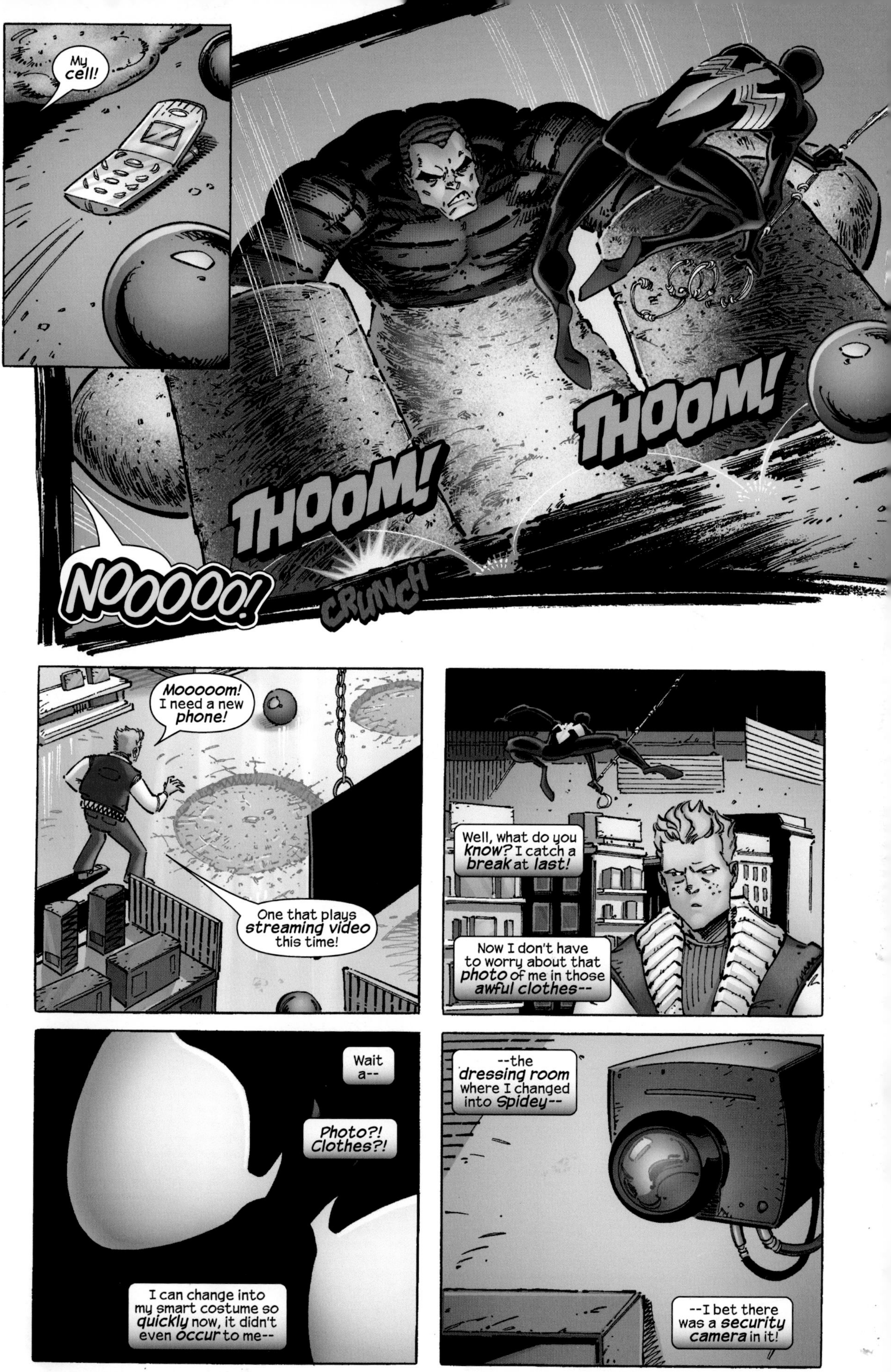
My cell!
THOOM!
THOOM!
NOOOOO!
CRUNCH
Moooom! I need a new phone!
One that plays streaming video this time!
Well, what do you know? I catch a break at last!
Now I don't have to worry about that photo of me in those awful clothes--
Wait a--
Photo?! Clothes?!
I can change into my smart costume so quickly now, it didn't even occur to me--
--the dressing room where I changed into Spidey--
--I bet there was a security camera in it!

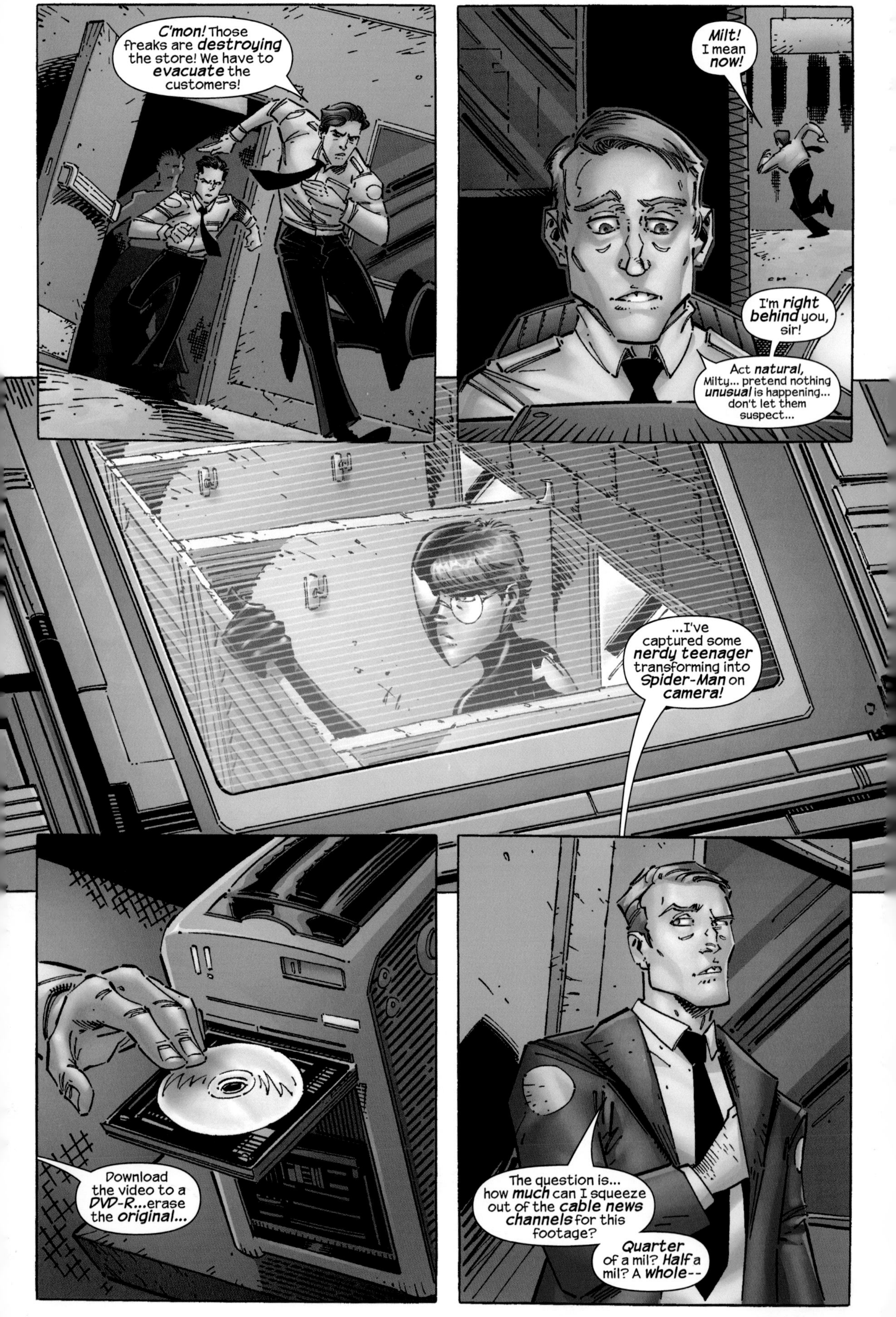
C'mon! Those freaks are destroying the store! We have to evacuate the customers!
Milt! I mean now!
I'm right behind you, sir!
Act natural, Milty... pretend nothing unusual is happening... don't let them suspect...
...I've captured some nerdy teenager transforming into Spider-Man on camera!
Download the video to a DVD-R...erase the original...
The question is... how much can I squeeze out of the cable news channels for this footage?
Quarter of a mil? Half a mil? A whole--

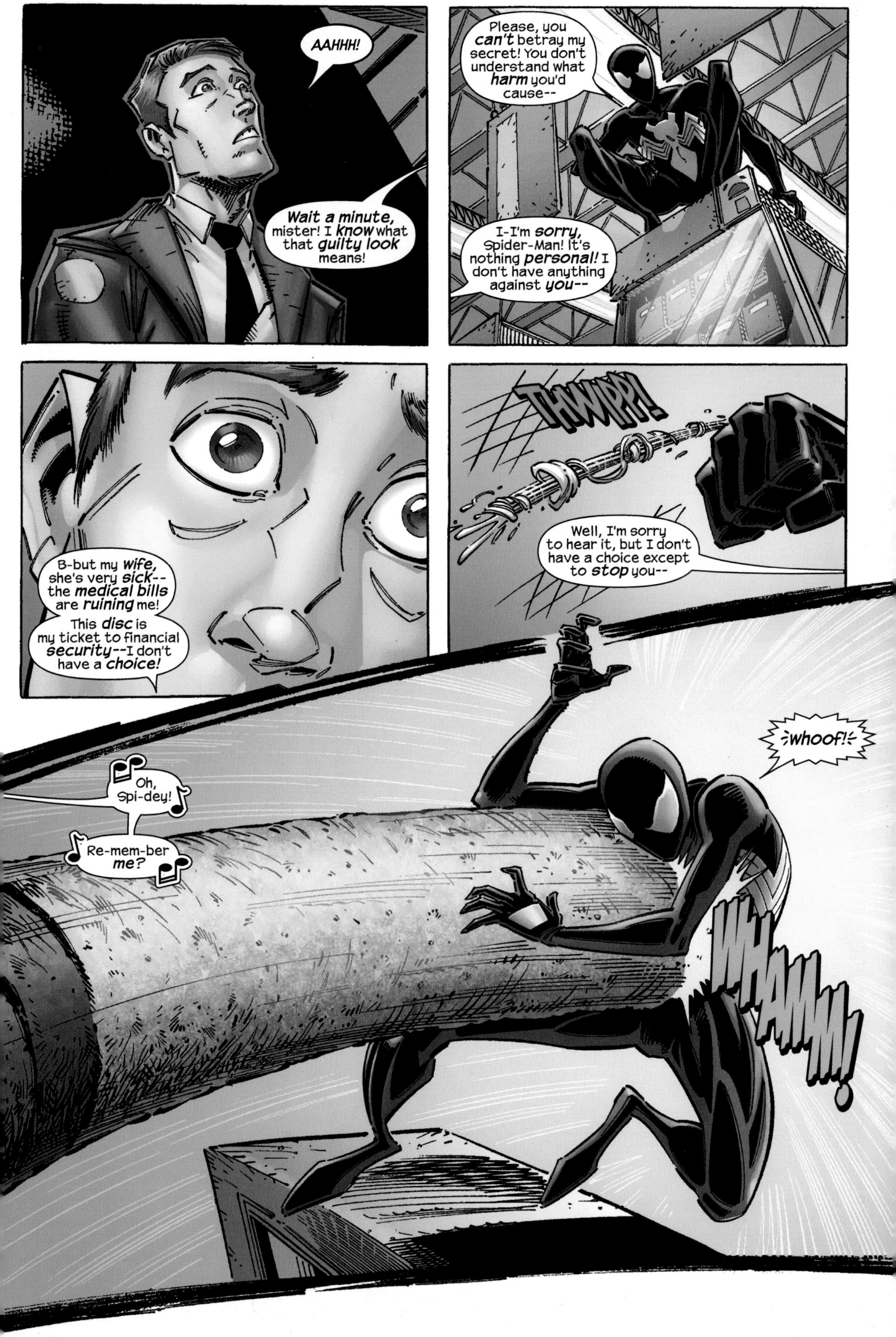

AAHHH!
Wait a minute, mister! I KNOW what that guilty look means!
Please, you can't betray my secret! You don't understand what harm you'd cause--
I-I'm sorry, Spider-Man! It's nothing personal! I don't have anything against you--
B-but my wife, she's very sick--the medical bills are ruining me!
This disc is my ticket to financial security--I don't have a choice!
THWIPP!
Well, I'm sorry to hear it, but I don't have a choice except to stop you--
whoof!
Oh, Spi-dey!
Re-mem-ber me?
WHAMM!

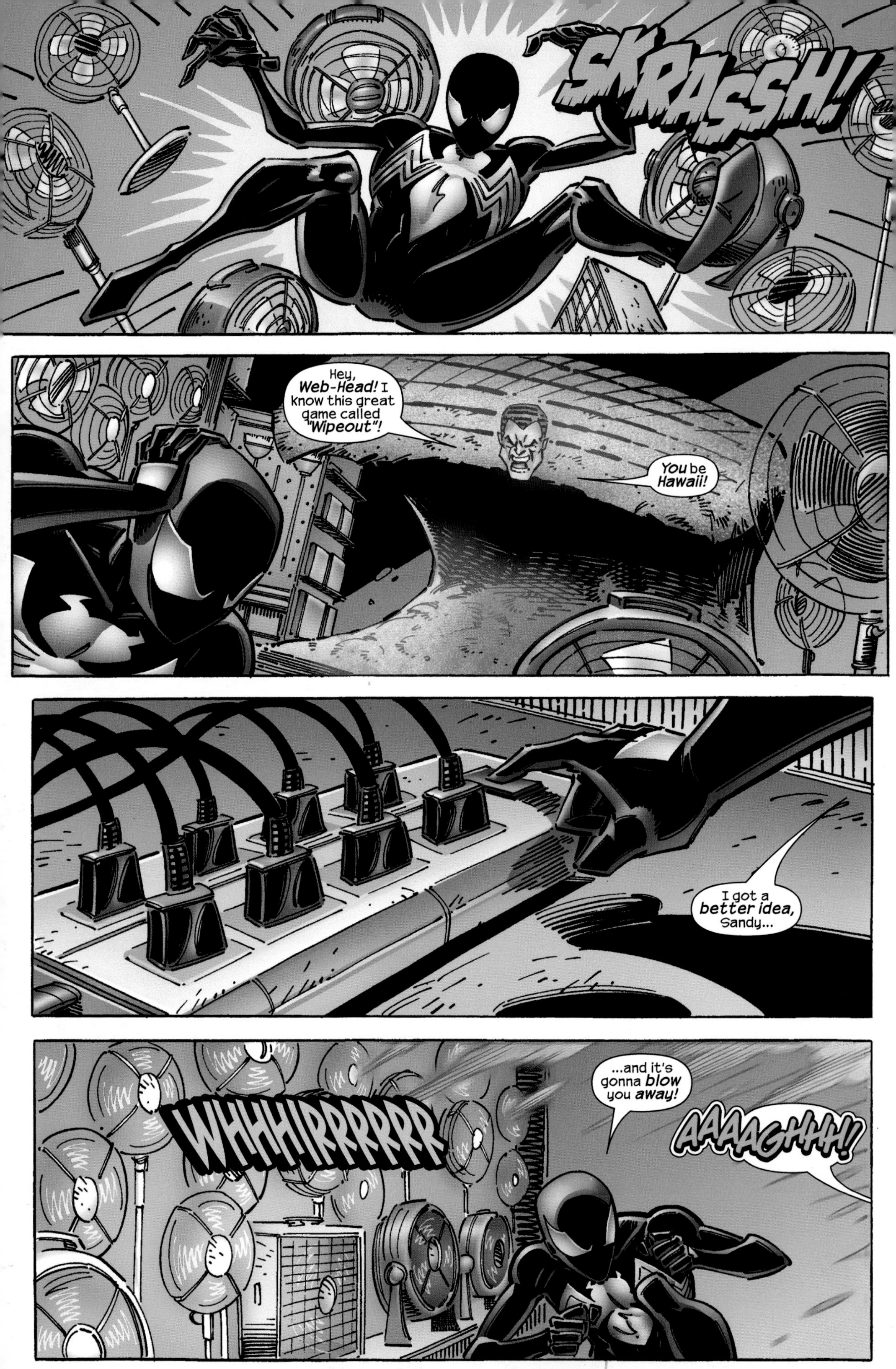
SKRASSH!
Hey, Web-Head! I know this great game called "Wipeout"!
You be Hawaii!
I got a better idea, Sandy...
WHHHIRRRRRR
...and it's gonna blow you away!
AAAAGHHH!

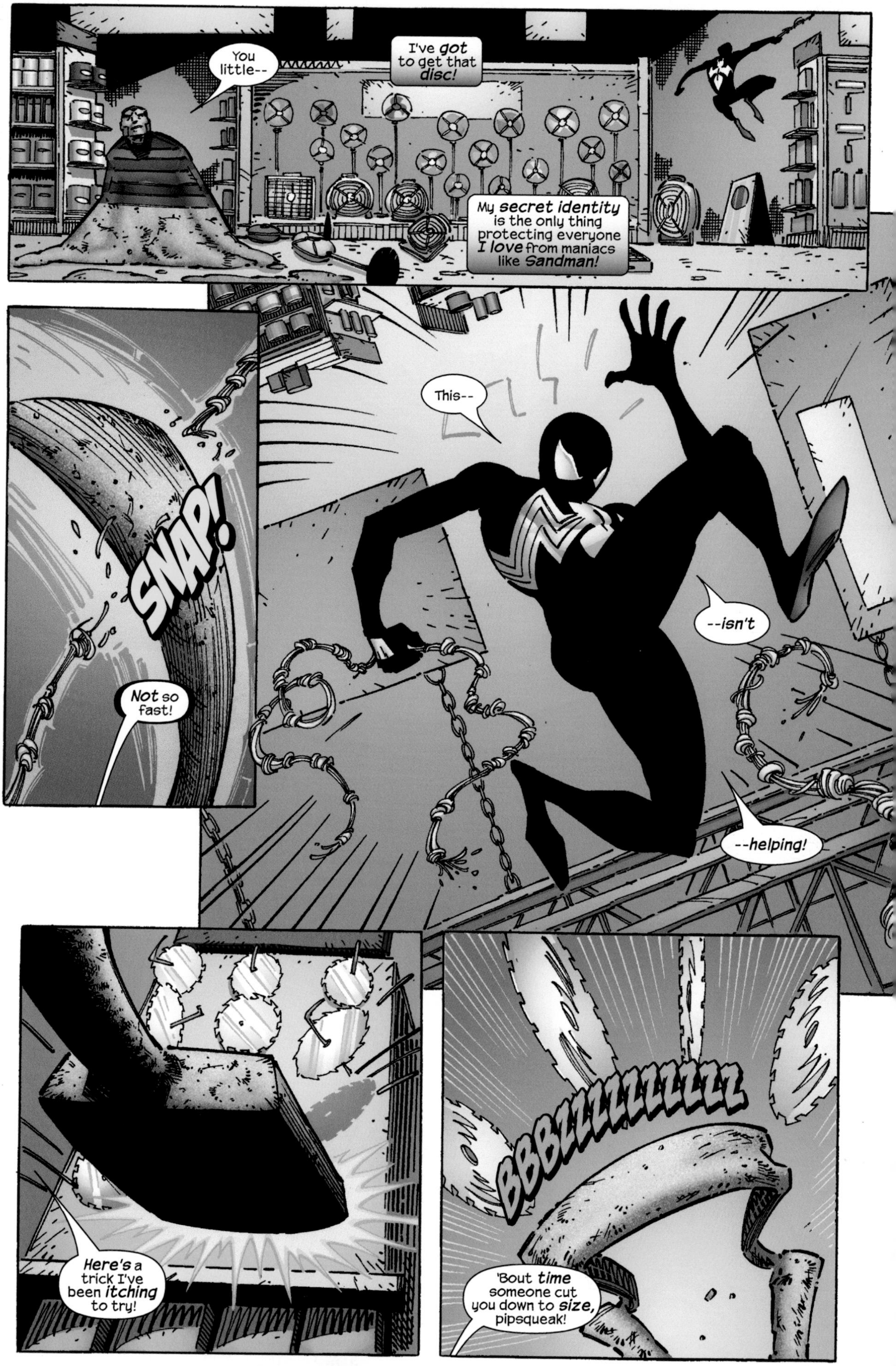

You little--
I've got to get that disc!
My secret identity is the only thing protecting everyone I love from maniacs like Sandman!
SNAP!
Not so fast!
This--
--isn't
--helping!
Here's a trick I've been itching to try!
BBBZZZZZZZZZZ
'Bout time someone cut you down to size, pipsqueak!

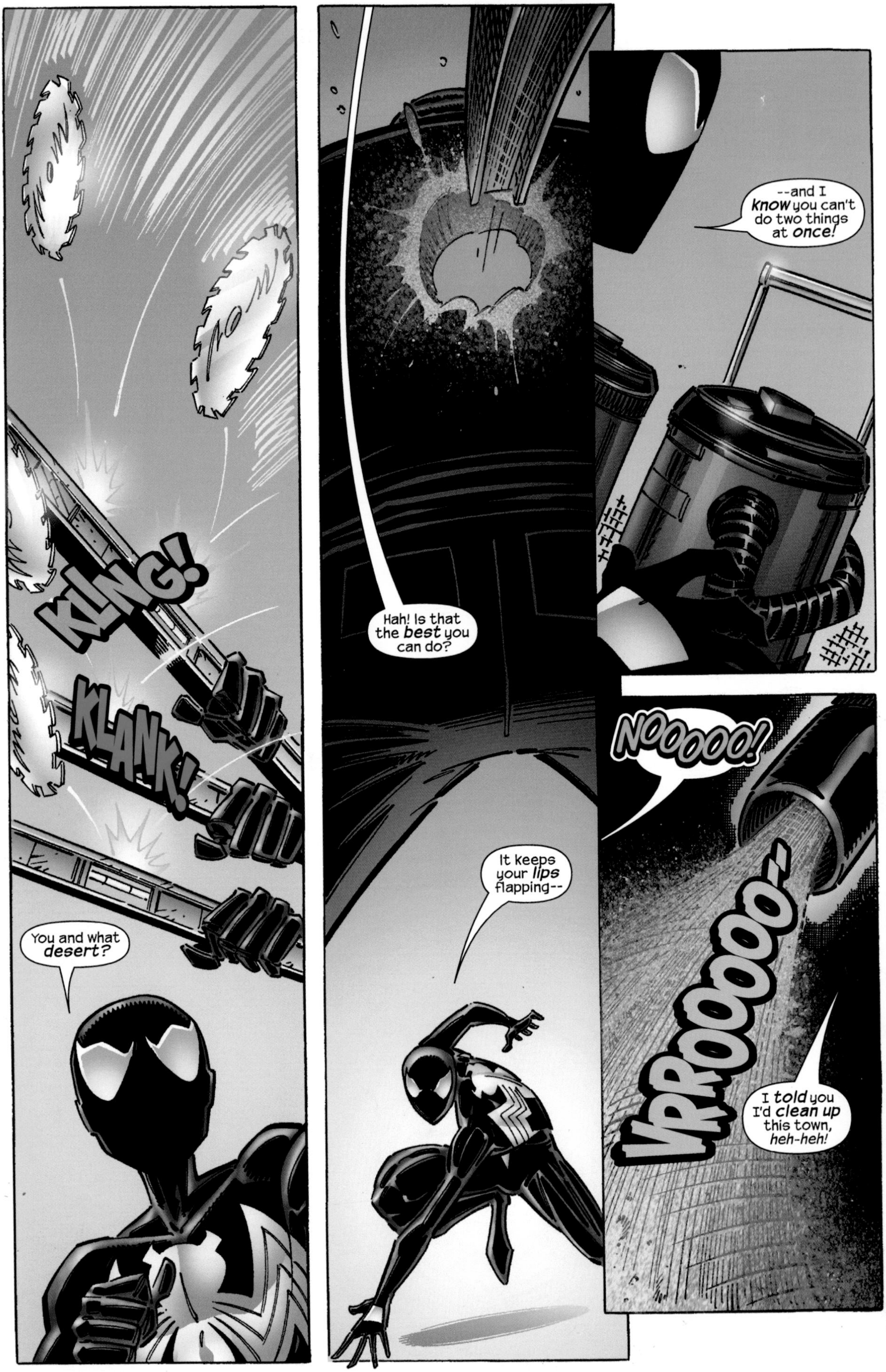

KLING!
KLANK!
You and what desert?
Hah! Is that the best you can do?
It keeps your lips flapping--
--and I know you can't do two things at once!
NOOOOO!
VRROOOOO--
I told you I'd clean up this town, heh-heh!

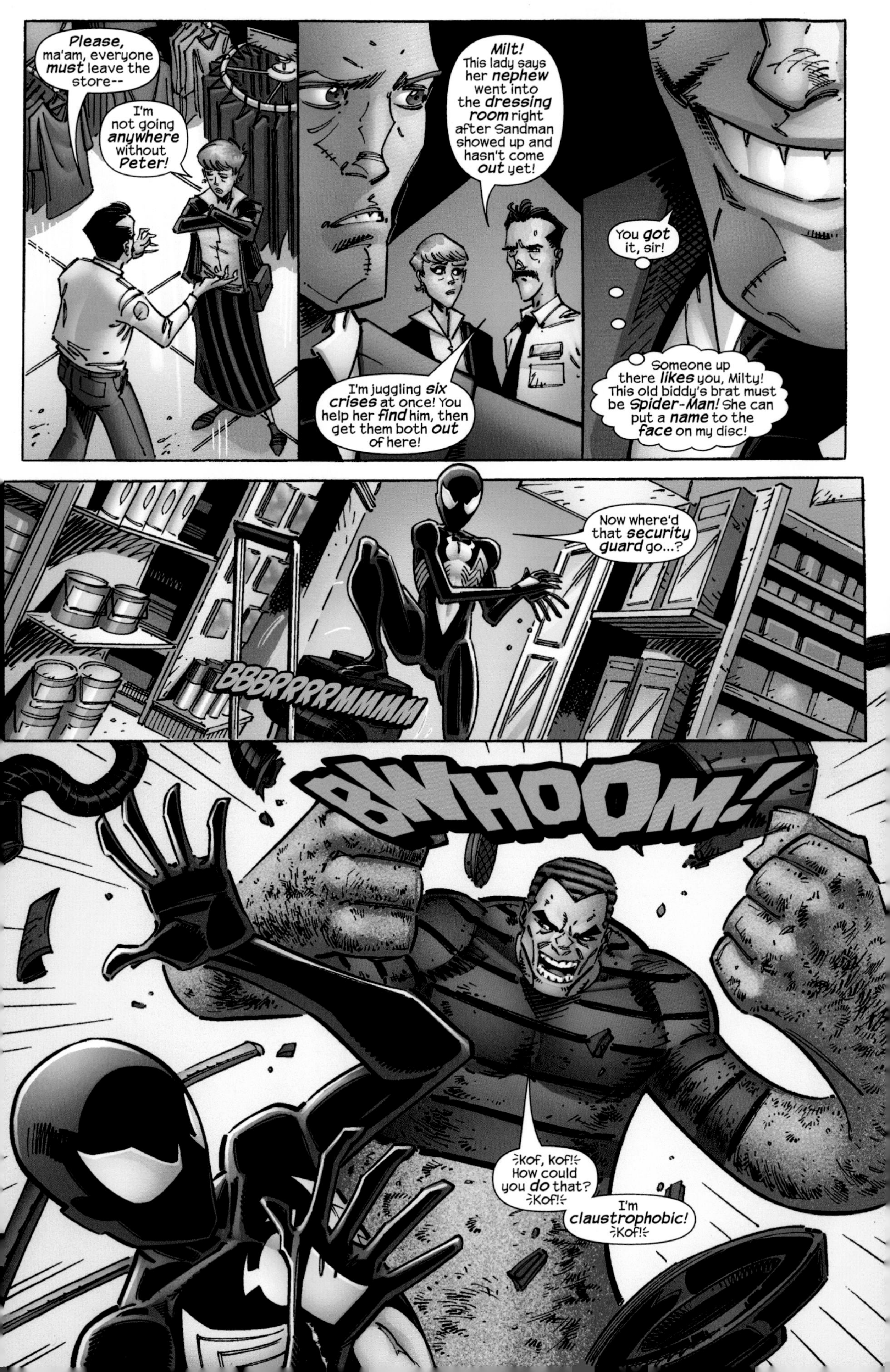
Please, ma'am, everyone must leave the store--
I'm not going anywhere without Peter!
Milt! This lady says her nephew went into the dressing room right after Sandman showed up and hasn't come out yet!
I'm juggling six crises at once! You help her find him, then get them both out of here!
You got it, sir!
Someone up there likes you, Milty! This old biddy's brat must be Spider-Man! She can put a name to the face on my disc!
Now where'd that security guard go...?
BBBRRRRMMMM
BWHOOM!
-Kof, kof!- How could you do that? -Kof!-
I'm claustrophobic! -Kof!-

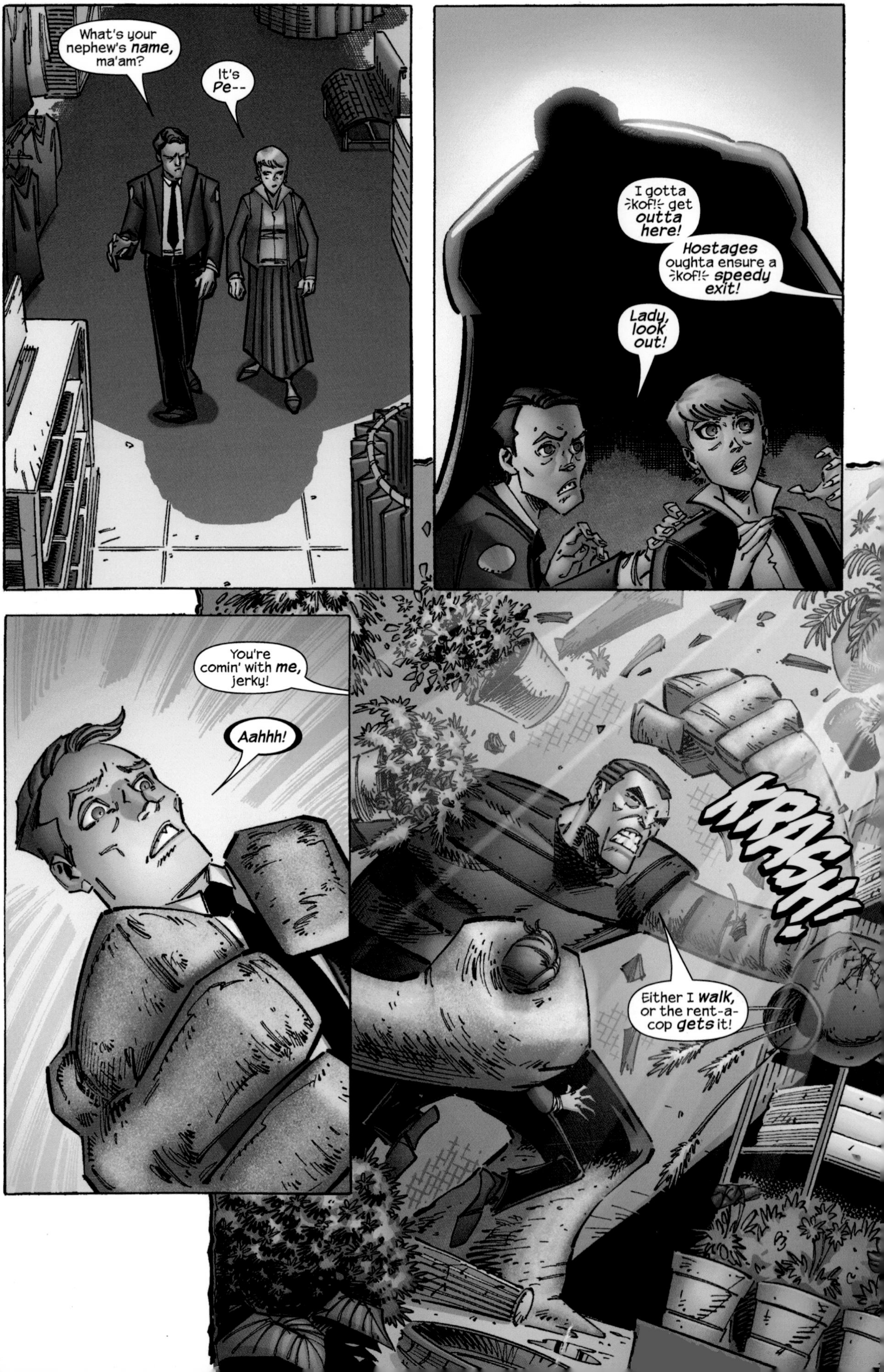

What's your nephew's name, ma'am?
It's Pe--
I gotta kof! get outta here!
Hostages oughta ensure a kof! speedy exit!
Lady, look out!
You're comin' with me, jerky!
Aahhh!
KRASH!
Either I walk, or the rent-a-cop gets it!

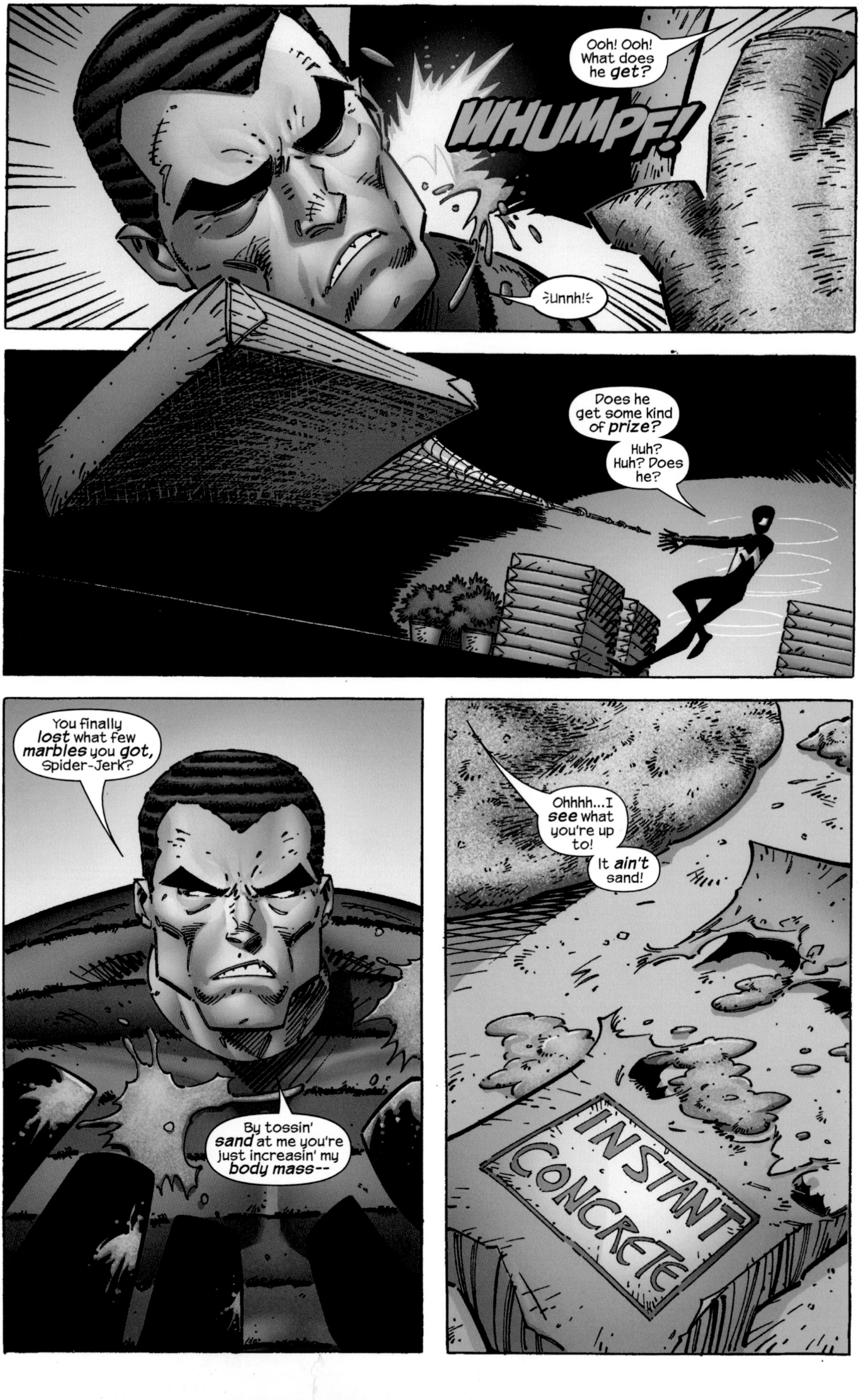
Ooh! Ooh! What does he get?
WHUMPF!
Unnh!
Does he get some kind of prize?
Huh? Huh? Does he?
You finally lost what few marbles you got, Spider-Jerk?
By tossin' sand at me you're just increasin' my body mass--
Ohhhh...I see what you're up to!
It ain't sand!
INSTANT CONCRETE

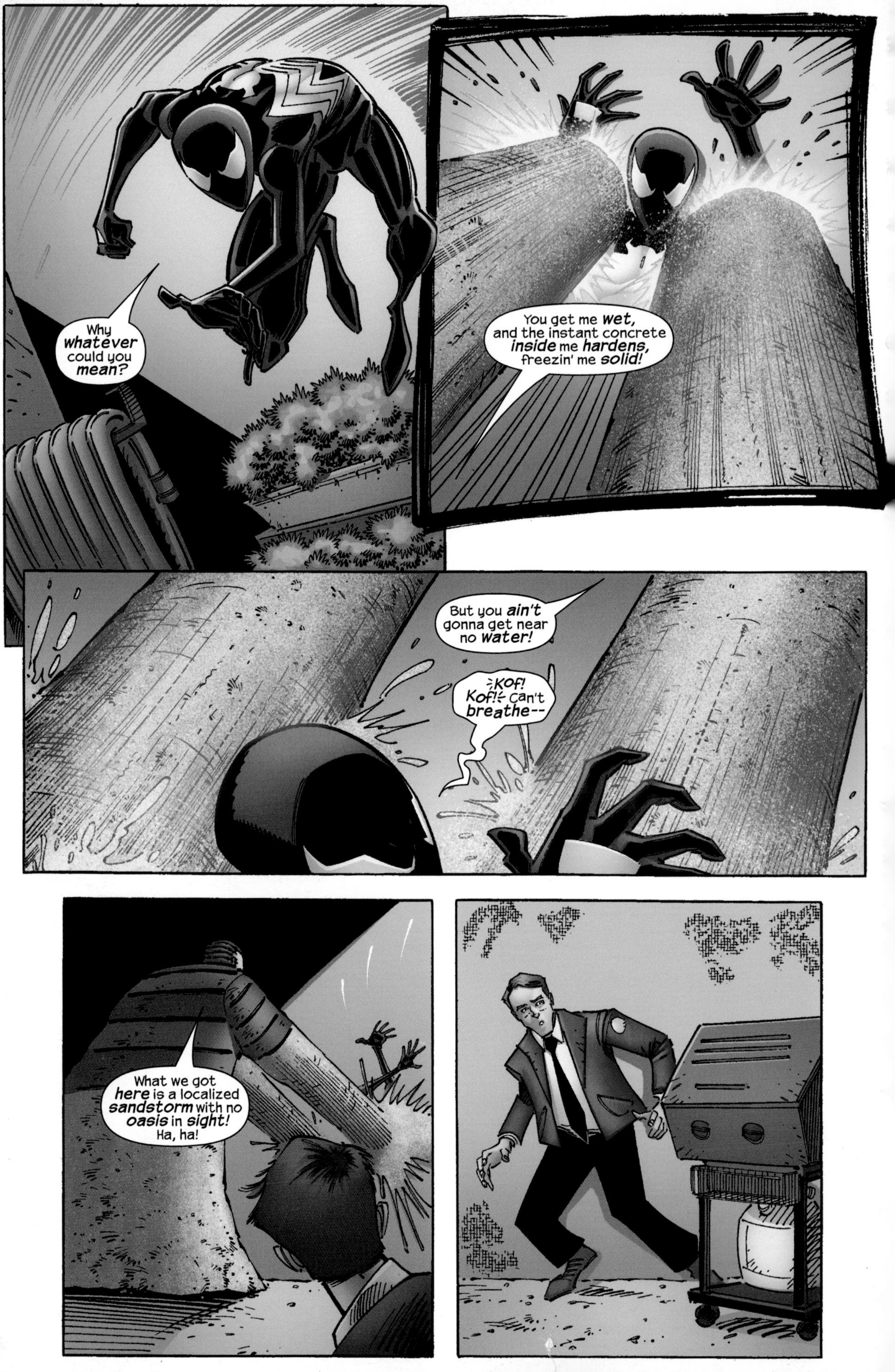
Why whatever could you mean?
You get me wet, and the instant concrete inside me hardens, freezin' me solid!
But you ain't gonna get near no water!
KOF! Kof! Can't breathe--
What we got here is a localized sandstorm with no oasis in sight! Ha, ha!

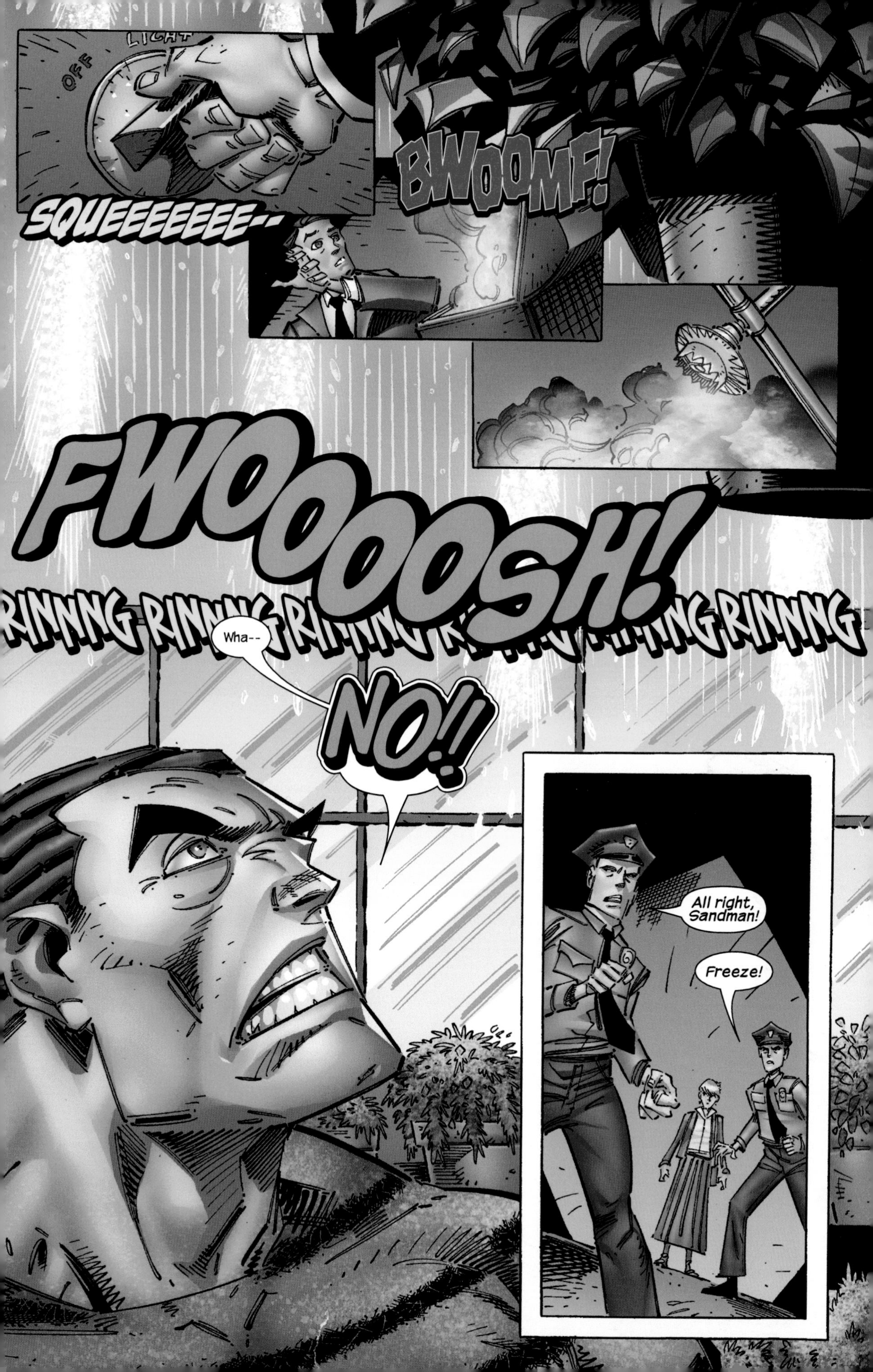

LIGHT
OFF
SQUEEEEEEEE--
BWOOMF!
FWOOOOSH!
RINNNG RINNNG
Wha--
NO!!
All right, Sandman!
Freeze!

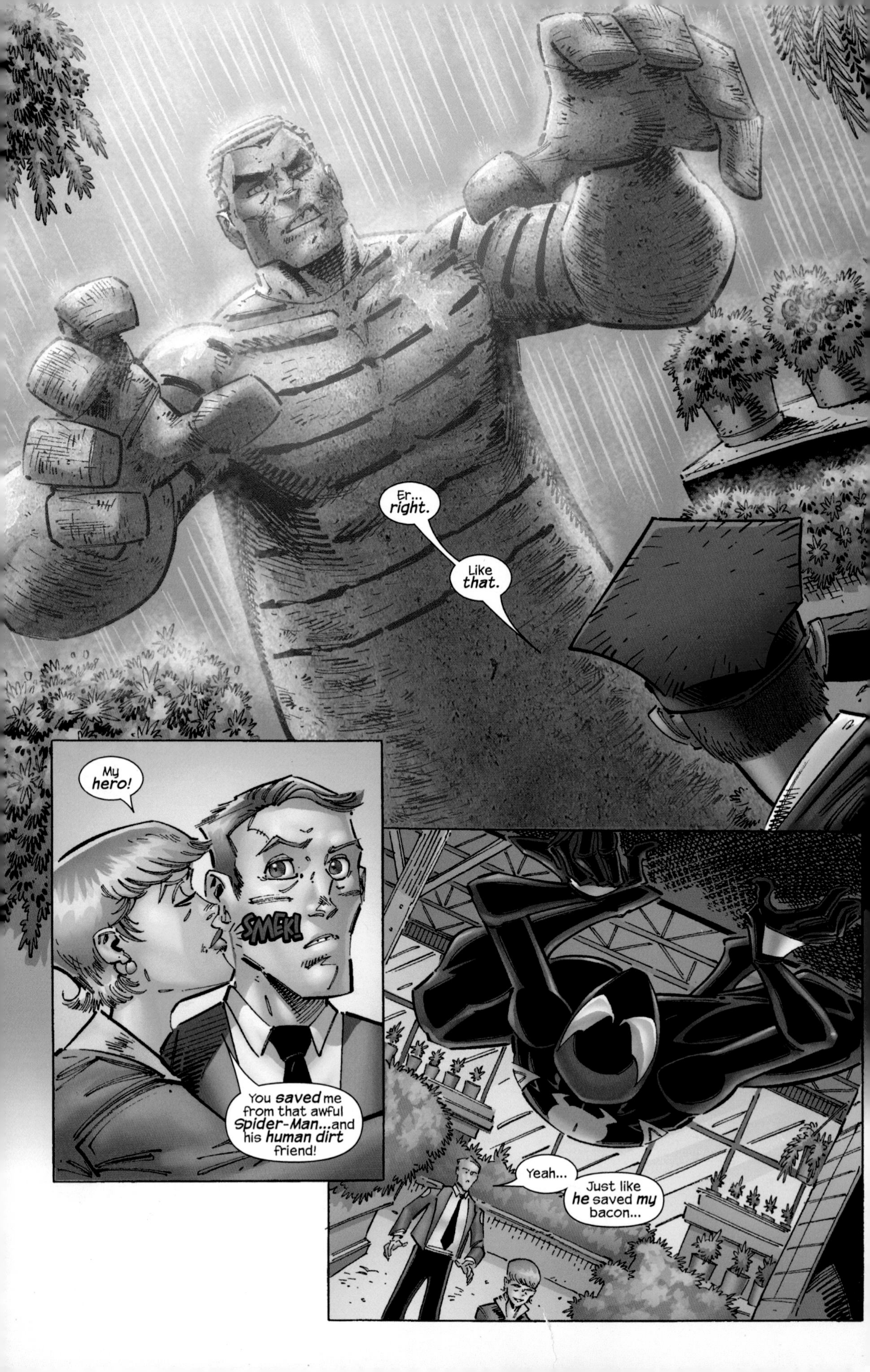
Er... right.
Like that.
My hero!
SMEK!
You saved me from that awful Spider-Man...and his human dirt friend!
Yeah...
Just like he saved my bacon...

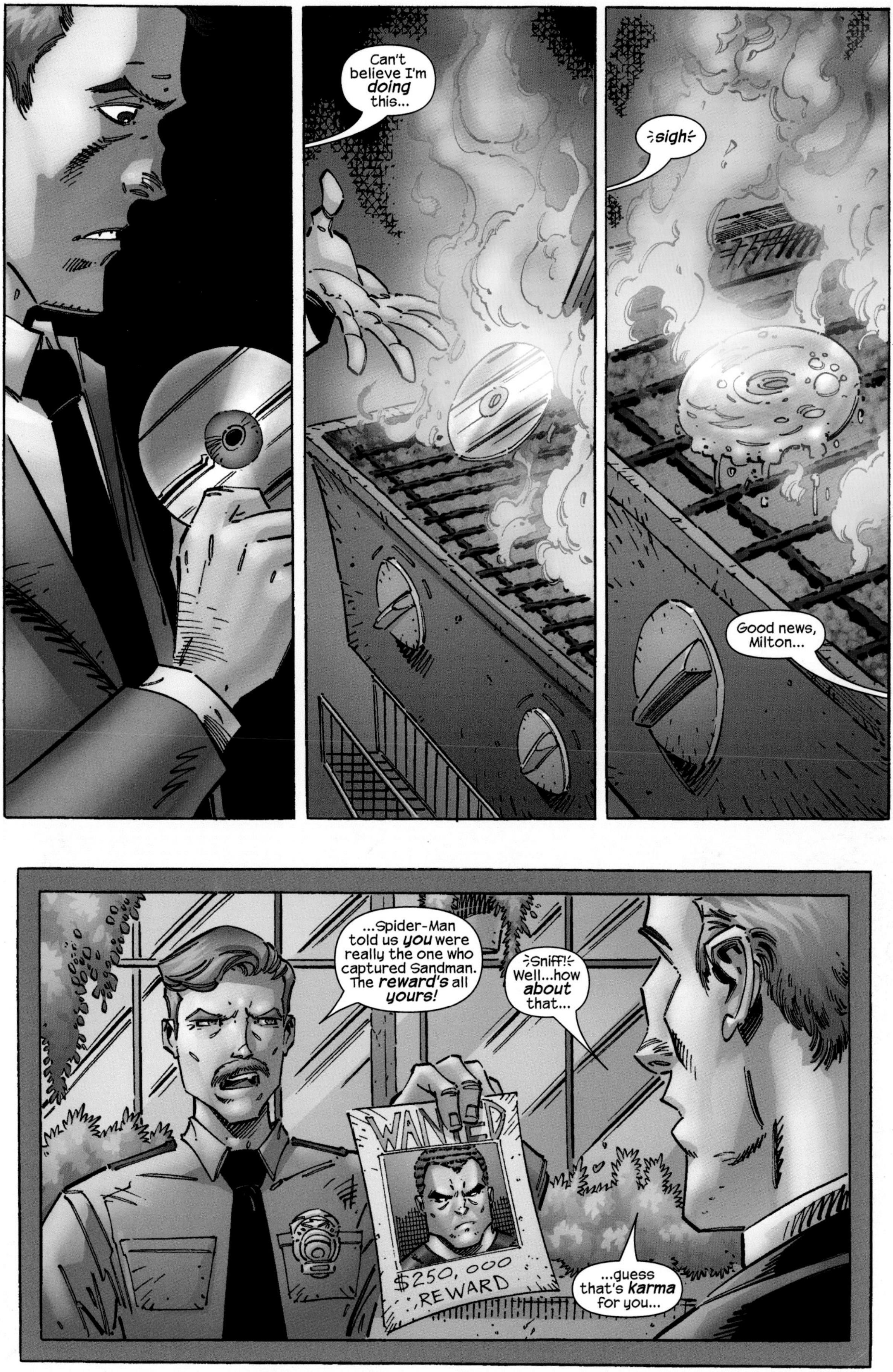
Can't believe I'm doing this...
sigh
Good news, Milton...
...Spider-Man told us you were really the one who captured Sandman. The reward's all yours!
Sniff! Well...how about that...
WANTED
$250,000 REWARD
...guess that's karma for you...

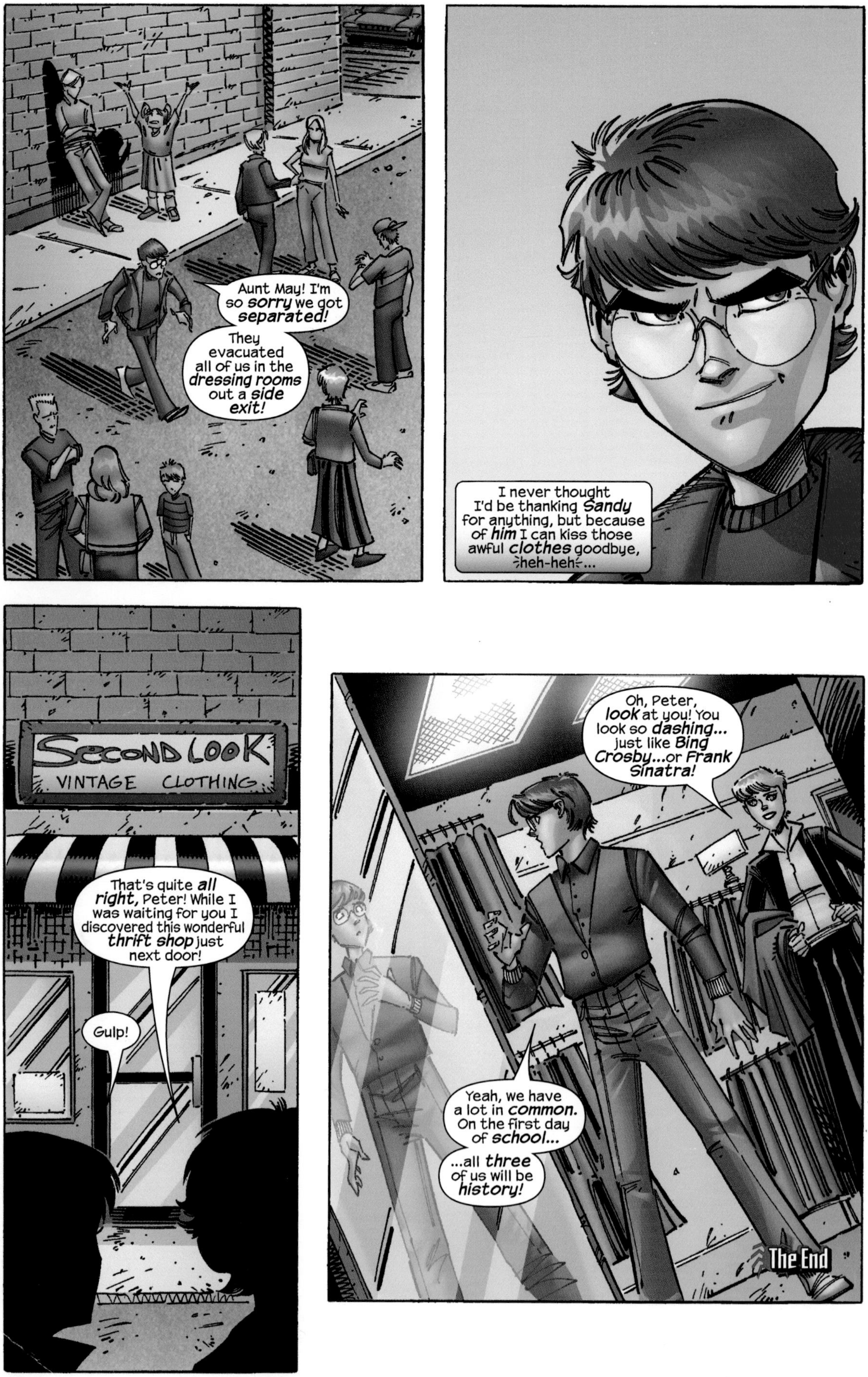
Aunt May! I'm so sorry we got separated!
They evacuated all of us in the dressing rooms out a side exit!
I never thought I'd be thanking Sandy for anything, but because of him I can kiss those awful clothes goodbye, heh-heh...
SECOND LOOK VINTAGE CLOTHING
That's quite all right, Peter! While I was waiting for you I discovered this wonderful thrift shop just next door!
Gulp!
Oh, Peter, look at you! You look so dashing... just like Bing Crosby...or Frank Sinatra!
Yeah, we have a lot in common. On the first day of school...
...all three of us will be history!
The End